IT'S THE BEAR!

For David, Amelia,
Jane, Jason, and Lucy
with thanks.

First published by Candlewick Press

CANDLEWICK PRESS
2067 MASSACHUSETTS AVENUE
CAMBRIDGE MA 02140

ISBN 0-590-62944-1

12 11 10 9 8   09 08 07 06 05 04 03 02

Printed in the U.S.A.   08

First Scholastic printing, April 1996

IT'S THE BEAR!

Jez Alborough

CANDLEWICK PRESS
CAMBRIDGE, MASSACHUSETTS

Eddie doesn't want to come
and picnic in the woods with Mom.

"I'm scared," he said, "about the bear,
the great big bear that lives in there."

"A bear?" said Mom. "That's silly, dear!
We don't get great big bears around here."

"There's just you and me and your teddy, Freddie.
Now let's all get the picnic ready."

"We've got lettuce,
   tomatoes, and
   cream cheese spread,
   with hard-boiled eggs
   and crusty brown bread.
   There's orange juice,
   cookies,
   some chips and—

      OH, MY!—

I've forgotten to pack
the blueberry pie . . . "

"I'll dash back and get it,"
she said. "Won't be long."
"BUT MOM!"
gasped Eddie . . .

too late—
SHE HAD GONE!

He sat on the basket
and tried not to cry.
Then . . .

"I CAN SMELL FOOD!"
yelled a voice
from nearby.

"*IT'S THE BEAR,*"
cried Eddie.
"*WHERE CAN I HIDE?*"

Then he opened
the basket and
clambered inside.

Out of the trees
stepped a big hungry bear,
licking his lips
and sniffing the air.
"A teddy bear's picnic,"
he bellowed. "Hooray!"
"Help," whispered Eddie.
"He's coming this way."

He cuddled
his teddy,
he huddled
and hid. . . .

Then a great big
bear bottom

sat down on the lid.

The bear munched
and he crunched.
He chomped
and he chewed,
and greedily gobbled up
all of the food.

"Now what's for dessert?" said the bear. "Let me see . . ."

"Oh, please," whimpered Eddie, "don't let it be me."

"Don't let him see me! *DON'T LET HIM COME ...*"

"Eddie, I'm coming," called Mom. "Are you hurt?"
"It's the bear," cried Eddie. "He thinks I'm dessert!"

"A bear?" said Mom. "I told you, my dear.
  Your Freddie's the only bear around here."

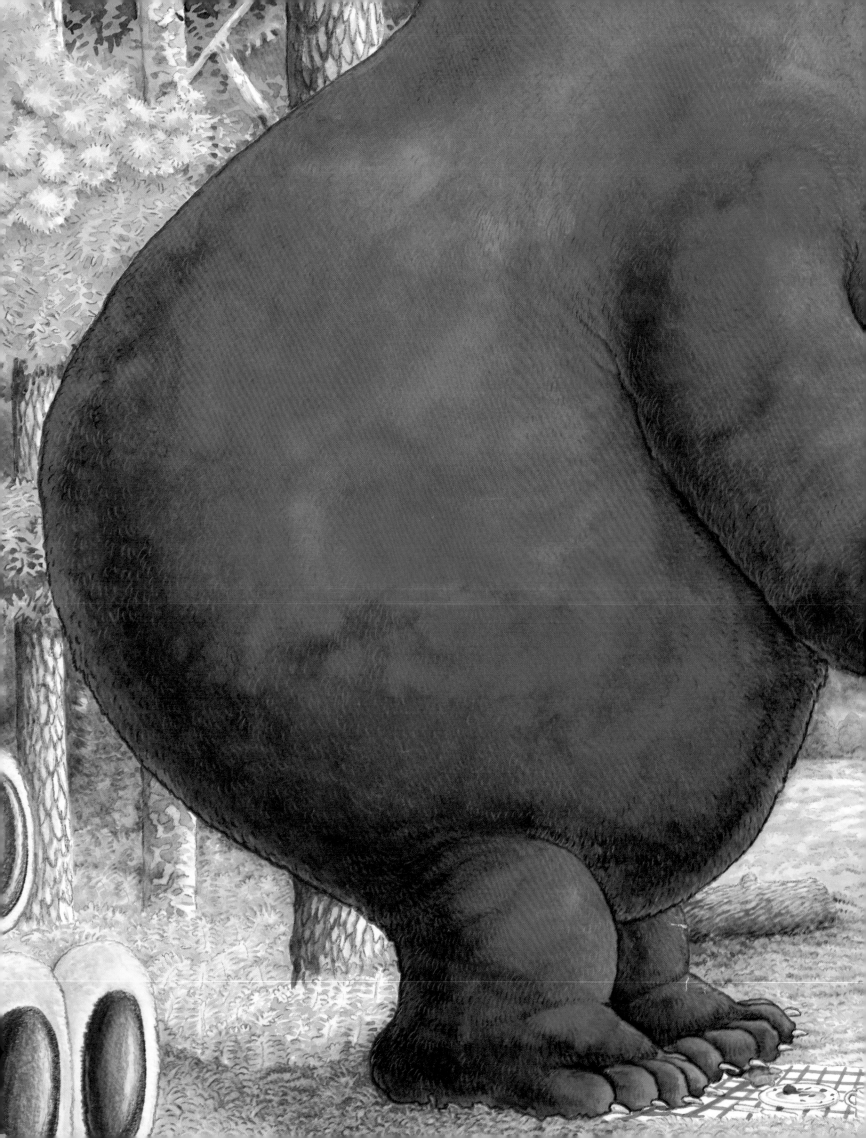

"NO HE'S NOT!" screamed Eddie. *"BEHIND YOU, HE'S THERE!"* "Don't be silly," said Mom. "There can't be . . . there just can't be . . . there isn't . . . "

"I *TOLD* you!" cried Eddie.
"*RUN!*" shouted Mom.
"Blueberry pie," said the bear.
"I *LOVE* it . . . "